Dear Parent:
Your child's love of reading starts here!

Every child learns to read in a different way and at his or her own speed. Some go back and forth between reading levels and read favorite books again and again. Others read through each level in order. You can help your young reader improve and become more confident by encouraging his or her own interests and abilities. From books your child reads with you to the first books he or she reads alone, there are I Can Read Books for every stage of reading:

SHARED READING
Basic language, word repetition, and whimsical illustrations, ideal for sharing with your emergent reader

BEGINNING READING
Short sentences, familiar words, and simple concepts for children eager to read on their own

READING WITH HELP
Engaging stories, longer sentences, and language play for developing readers

READING ALONE
Complex plots, challenging vocabulary, and high-interest topics for the independent reader

I Can Read Books have introduced children to the joy of reading since 1957. Featuring award-winning authors and illustrators and a fabulous cast of beloved characters, I Can Read Books set the standard for beginning readers.

A lifetime of discovery begins with the magical words "I Can Read!"

Visit www.icanread.com for information
on enriching your child's reading experience.

I Can Read® and I Can Read Book® are trademarks of HarperCollins Publishers.

The Adventures of Paddington: Paddington and the Painting

Based on the Paddington novels written and created by Michael Bond
PADDINGTON™ and PADDINGTON BEAR™ © Paddington and Company/Studiocanal S.A.S. 2020
Paddington Bear™, Paddington™, and PB™ are trademarks of Paddington and Company Limited
Licensed on behalf of Studiocanal S.A.S. by Copyrights Group
www.paddington.com

ISBN 978-0-06-298307-7 (trade bdg)—ISBN 978-0-06-298306-0 (pbk.)

20 21 22 23 24 LSCC 10 9 8 7 6 5 4 3 2 1 ❖ First Edition

My First SHARED READING

I Can Read!

The Adventures of
Paddington™
Paddington and the Painting

Based on the episode "Paddington and the Painting"

by Jon Foster and James Lamont

Adapted by Alyssa Satin Capucilli

HARPER

An Imprint of HarperCollinsPublishers

In this story you will meet:

Paddington: He loves his aunt Lucy and writes her lots of letters. He also loves sweet orange jam called marmalade.

Mrs. Brown: She is an artist. She loves to paint!

Mr. Curry: He lives next door to the Browns.

4

Paddington wanted to help
Mrs. Brown.

Dear Aunt Lucy,
Today is the art show.
We are going to see
Mrs. Brown's painting!

Paddington was enjoying
his breakfast.
Just then, Mrs. Brown came in.

"I can't be in the art s
It's tonight.
I don't know what to p

"Don't give up,"
said Paddington.

Paddington looked
at Mrs. Brown's paintings.
"I like this horse!" he said.

"That's a fish," said Mrs. Brown.
"These are no good
for the art show."

"Let's start over,"
said Paddington.
He picked up a brush.
He painted one dot.

"Now it's your turn," he said.
Mrs. Brown looked at the dot.
She still didn't know
what to paint.

"Let's try something else,"
said Paddington.
He covered his eyes.
Then he covered
Mrs. Brown's eyes, too.

They tossed paint here!
They tossed paint there!

There was paint on the walls.
There was paint on the floor.
But there was no paint
on the painting!

So there was still no painting for the art show.

"I need to think,"
said Mrs. Brown.
She did some yoga.
She thought and thought.

Paddington did yoga, too.

He thought and thought.

He fell asleep.

"Oh no," said Mrs. Brown.
"I don't know what to do."
She looked sad.

So Paddington and Mrs. Brown
walked in the garden.
"You can paint a tree
or a flower," said Paddington.

"I have to paint something
amazing," said Mrs. Brown.

"Look at what Mr. Curry
is making, Mrs. Brown,"
said Paddington.

"That is amazing,"
said Mrs. Brown.
"But not for my painting."

"Maybe a snack will help
us think," said Paddington.
"I love spaghetti!"
Paddington ate and ate.
The spaghetti was very long!

"Now I know what to paint,"
said Mrs. Brown with a smile.
"I will paint you, Paddington.
You are an amazing bear."

Paddington posed
for Mrs. Brown.
She painted and painted.

Soon the painting was ready
for the art show.
And it even won a prize!

Dear Aunt Lucy,

Today I learned to paint.

It's fun to use a brush . . .

or even a paw!

Love from Paddington